Ziggy Marley

My Dog Romeo

Yo, that's my dog.
That's my real dog.
Yo what's up, my dog?
That's my dog Romeo.

Yo, yo, Romeo,
why you chewin' on the mic stand?

My dog

ROMEO

C'mon man!

My dog Romeo.
My dog Romeo.

Send a shout-out
and big up now,
that's my dog Romeo.

I have two legs.
My friend, he has four.
He likes to stop, and I like to go.

I like to smell the flowers.
He likes to smell the floors.
He is really fast
for just twelve weeks old.

He wakes me in the morning,
six o'clock sharp.

I take him out to potty
and he rolls in the grass.

He loves to meet people
when they come to the door.

And when I play my guitar,
he chills on the floor!

Send a shout-out and big up
now to my dog Romeo.
My dog Romeo.
That's my dog Romeo.
Send a shout-out and big up
now, that's my dog Romeo.

He always gives affection

He always gets LOVE

Sometimes he pretends that he is a wild animal.

He running through the bushes
with a bone in his mouth.

When he's done running the bushes
then he's knocking at the door.

We'll take him for a walk
to get his mind real clear.

And sometimes he's the one
who wants to take you somewhere.

Hey Romeo, where you going?
No, this way.
Yeah, c'mon boy.
Good boy, good boy, good boy!

My dog Romeo.
My dog Romeo.
Send a shout-out and big up
now to my dog Romeo.

My dog Romeo.

My dog Romeo.

Send a shout-out and big up now
to my dog
Romeo.

My dog Romeo,
that's my dog Romeo.
Send a shout-out and big up
now to the dogs all around.

My dog Romeo,
that's my dog Romeo.
Send a shout-out and big up
now to all the dogs all around . . .

Words by Ziggy Marley
Illustrations by Ag Jatkowska

Executive produced by Tuff Gong Worldwide

© 2021 Tuff Gong Worldwide, LLC
© 2020 "My Dog Romeo" lyrics published by Ishti
    Music, Inc.

Published by Akashic Books/
    Tuff Gong Worldwide Books
ISBN-13: 978-1-61775-942-0
Library of Congress Control Number: 2020948050

First printing
Printed in China

Akashic Books
Brooklyn, New York
Twitter: @AkashicBooks
Facebook: AkashicBooks
E-mail: info@akashicbooks.com
Website: www.akashicbooks.com

TUFF GONG
WORLDWIDE

AKASHIC
BOOKS

ZIGGY MARLEY is an eight-time **GRAMMY** Award winner, Emmy Award winner, author, philanthropist, and reggae icon. He has released thirteen albums to much critical acclaim, and is the author of three other children's books: *I Love You Too*, *Music Is in Everything*, and *Little John Crow* (with his wife Orly Marley); as well the *Ziggy Marley and Family Cookbook*. His early immersion in music came at age ten when he sat in on recording sessions with his father, Bob Marley. Ziggy Marley and the Melody Makers released eight best-selling albums that garnered three **GRAMMY**s. Ziggy's second solo release, *Love Is My Religion*, won a **GRAMMY** in 2006 for Best Reggae Album. His third solo studio album, *Family Time*, scored a fifth **GRAMMY** award for Best Children's Album. 2016 marked the release of Marley's self-titled album, which earned his eighth **GRAMMY**. Marley's new children's album, *More Family Time*, was released in September 2020 via Tuff Gong Worldwide.

Also available from Ziggy Marley

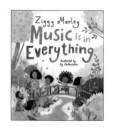

MUSIC IS IN EVERYTHING by Ziggy Marley • Illustrations by Ag Jatkowska
A children's picture book • Forthcoming fall 2021

A picture book based on Ziggy Marley's popular song celebrating music's many forms, from the sounds of ocean waves to laughter in the family kitchen.

LITTLE JOHN CROW by Ziggy Marley and Orly Marley
Illustrations by Gordon Rowe
A children's picture book • Forthcoming fall 2021

After being abandoned by his animal friends, Little John Crow must come to terms with what it means to be part of a community when you are a vulture.

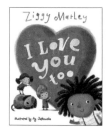

I LOVE YOU TOO by Ziggy Marley • Illustrations by Ag Jatkowska
A children's picture book

"A sweetly affectionate ode to togetherness and love." —*Publishers Weekly*

"Sure to be a hit at bedtime, the lyrical story conveys the sweet, soothing, and affirming message." —*School Library Journal*

ZIGGY MARLEY AND FAMILY COOKBOOK

"[Ziggy's] first collection of recipes pays homage to the flavors of his youth and the food he loves to cook for his wife and five children." —*People*

"With a health-focused approach, Ziggy Marley reveals memories and food traditions in his new family cookbook." —*Ebony*